3 Beloved Tales

Beauty and the Beast

Stories Around the World

by Cari Meister

PICTURE WINDOW BOOKS

a capstone imprint

What Is a Fairy Tale?

Once upon a time, before the age of books, people gathered to tell stories. They told tales of fairies and magic, princes and witches. Ideas of love, jealousy, kindness, and luck filled the stories. Some provided lessons. Others just entertained. Most did both! These fairy tales passed from neighbor to neighbor, village to village, land to land. As the stories spun across seas and over mountains, details changed to fit each culture. A poisoned apple became a poisoned ring. A king became a sultan. A wolf became a tiger.

Over time, fairy tales were collected and written down. Around the world today, people of all ages love to read or hear these timeless stories. For many years to come, fairy tales will continue to live happily ever after in our imaginations.

Beauty and the Beast
A French Fairy Tale

illustrated by
Colleen Madden

Once there was a rich merchant who had three daughters. The two oldest daughters were selfish and greedy. The youngest, named Beauty, was kind and good. One day misfortune struck. The merchant lost everything except a small house in the country. Beauty's sisters did nothing but grumble. Beauty, on the other hand, kept a cheerful spirit.

After a year the merchant received news: one of his ships had returned safely to harbor.

"Thank goodness!" cried Beauty's sisters. "Our wretched life will soon end!"

3

As the merchant saddled his horse, he asked what he should bring back.

"Gowns and ribbons!" demanded his eldest daughters.

"Your safe return," said Beauty.

The merchant smiled. "Of course," he said. "Is there anything else?"

"A single red rose," replied Beauty.

The merchant went to the city. But alas! His ship's goods were sold to pay outstanding debts. Sadly, he started home. Soon a terrible snowstorm made it terribly hard to see. He lost his way in the woods. Cold and tired, he wandered until he stumbled onto a hidden castle.

He knocked on the door, but no one answered. Fearing death if he did not warm up, the merchant opened the door. Inside, a giant fire roared. Near the fire was a fine plate of food. Thankful, the merchant ate and fell asleep.

The next morning he discovered a rose garden. Thinking of Beauty, he selected a beautiful red rose. Suddenly a hideous beast appeared.

"Ungrateful wretch!" roared the beast. "I gave you food and shelter. This is how you repay me—by stealing what I value most!"

"I'm terribly sorry," cried the merchant. "You see, my youngest daughter asked for a rose, and these are so lovely—please forgive—"

"Silence!" demanded Beast. "I'll forgive you if one of your daughters comes to the palace to live with me. But she must come of her own free will."

The merchant froze in terror.

Beast continued, "If someone doesn't come within three months, I'll come for you, and you shall live in my dungeon."

The poor merchant! How could he send one of his daughters to live with a monster?

When the merchant returned home, he told his daughters what had happened.

His oldest daughters were shocked. "You expect us to live with a beast?" they asked. "Never!"

But Beauty looked kindly upon her father.

"I'll go," she said.

So Beauty went to the palace, certain the beast planned to eat her. To her surprise, he was gentle and kind, smart and generous.

Beauty enjoyed Beast's company. But every day he asked, "Will you marry me?" Every day Beauty replied, "You're a dear friend, but I cannot be your wife."

This happened for months.

One day, Beast asked Beauty why she looked sad.

"I miss my father," she said. "I'd like to see him."

Beast let her go. "But if you don't return," he said, "I'll surely die of a broken heart."

Beast gave her a ring. "When you want to return to me, simply put on the ring," he told her.

Beauty threw her arms around Beast. "Thank you!" she replied.

Oh, how happy Beauty's father was to see her! They sang and danced. Weeks flew by, but Beauty missed Beast. For in her heart, she realized that she had come to love him. That night she put on the ring. When she woke, she found herself in the castle, but Beast was nowhere to be found.

"Where are you?" Beauty cried.

There was no answer.

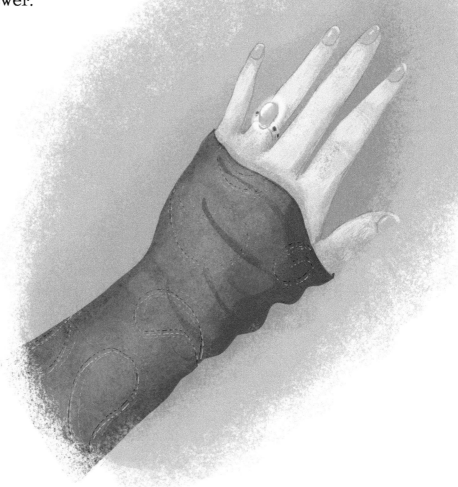

At last, Beauty found him in the rose garden. He was near death.

"Oh, Beast! What have I done?" cried Beauty. "I do want to be your wife. I love you!"

With these words, the palace sparkled and the beast disappeared. In his place was a handsome prince.

"You've broken the enchantment!" he said. "You loved me for who I am, not how I looked."

Soon they were married. They lived happily ever after.

The Fairy Serpent

A Chinese Fairy Tale illustrated by Iva Sasheva

Long ago in China lived a man and his three daughters.
Every day on his way home from work, he would stop and
gather flowers. The girls would use the flowers in their
embroidery patterns. One day he couldn't find any flowers
on the path, so he ventured into the woods. Suddenly
a fairy serpent coiled around him.

"How dare you enter my garden!" hissed the serpent.

"I beg your forgiveness," said the man. "I was only looking for a few flowers for my daughters."

This caught the serpent's attention.

"How many daughters have you?" he asked.

When the man told him, the serpent gripped tighter.

"I'll let you go, if you promise that you'll send one to marry me," the serpent said.

Repulsed, the man offered the serpent other things, but the serpent would accept nothing else. Finally, the man agreed and hurried home.

The man was so distraught that he couldn't eat. Finally, one by one, his daughters tried to figure out what was wrong.

The oldest daughter went first. "Bá," she said. "We're worried. What's wrong?"

Her father told her about the promise he had made to the serpent.

"Will you, for my sake, marry the serpent?" he asked.

"No!" she said.

15

The middle daughter was next. "Bá," she said. "We're worried. What's wrong?"

Again, the father told his story.

"Will you marry the serpent?" he asked.

"No!" she, too, replied.

The youngest daughter went last.
"Bá," she said. "Why haven't you eaten?"

For the third time, he explained his promise to the serpent.

"Will you marry the snake?" he asked.

"If you promise you'll eat again," she said. "I'll go when he calls for me."

So the father ate. And for a few days, everything was fine.

Then, one morning, as the girls were embroidering, a wasp flew in.

"I buzz and sting. Fast and faster. Who will wed my serpent master?" sang the wasp.

The girls chased the wasp away.

The next morning two wasps came.

"We buzz and sting, faster and faster. Who will wed our serpent master?" they sang.

Again, the girls shooed the wasps away.

The next day a swarm of wasps appeared and the youngest daughter knew she could delay no longer.

She said farewell to her family and followed the wasps.

The fairy serpent was waiting for her outside a splendid palace. Inside, there was beautiful furniture and chests full of silk, jade, and gold. It was everything anyone could ask for.

The girl was surprised but thankful for the serpent's thoughtfulness.

During the wedding dinner she said, "Thank you for everything. I'll try to be a good wife for you."

For several weeks the girl did everything she could for her husband. The serpent treated her like a queen. Soon the girl grew to love having the serpent around. She was sad when he couldn't be near.

One day she found the well dry. She went to the far part of the forest to find water. It was hard to carry that big bucket of water, but she knew her husband needed it.

When she returned, she found the snake dying.
Quickly, she splashed him with water.

"Please don't die," she whimpered. "I love you."

Magically, the snake transformed into a handsome man.

"Thank you," he said, kissing his bride. "I was under
a spell, but your love has set me free."

The Bear Prince

A Swiss Fairy Tale illustrated by Marieke Nelissen

One day a merchant was going to market.

"What would you like me to bring back?" he asked his daughters.

The eldest daughter answered, "Pearls."

The middle daughter said, "A new blue dress."

The youngest daughter answered simply, "A grape."

At the market the merchant immediately found pearls and a blue dress. But he couldn't find a single grape. This made him sad, because he loved his youngest daughter most of all.

As he walked home, a dwarf walked up beside him. "Why are you so sad?"

"My daughter wanted a grape, and I couldn't find a single one."

"You're in luck!" said the dwarf, pointing. "Go down to that meadow. You'll see a vineyard and a white bear. Don't be afraid of the bear. He will give you a grape."

So the merchant went down to the meadow
and found the bear.

"What do you want?" growled the bear.

"Only a single grape for my daughter," said
the merchant.

"You can have one," said the bear, "as long as
you give me that which first greets you when
you return home."

The merchant didn't think too much of the bear's
request and agreed. The bear gave him the largest,
juiciest grape. The merchant was happy.

When he got home, his youngest daughter rushed out to greet him. She always missed him while he was away. She thanked him for the beautiful grape and hugged him tightly.

The merchant was heartbroken. He wondered when the bear would take away his precious daughter.

Exactly one year later, the bear appeared. "Give me that which first greeted you when you returned home."

The merchant said, "It was my dog."

The bear growled, for he knew the merchant was lying. "Keep your promise, or I'll eat you!"

The merchant tried again. "Take the apple tree, then. It was the first thing I touched."

This time, when the bear growled, he showed his teeth. "Keep your promise, or I'll eat you this instant!"

27

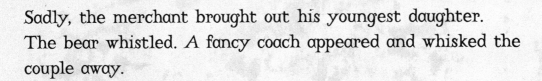

Sadly, the merchant brought out his youngest daughter.
The bear whistled. A fancy coach appeared and whisked the
couple away.

The girl was surprised when she arrived at a beautiful castle.

"This is your home now," said the bear kindly.

The bear gave his new wife everything she could ever want. After a while the girl hardly noticed that her husband was a bear. She came to love him very much.

There was only one strange rule in the castle: no lights at night.

After one year the bear took his wife to see her father. The merchant was excited to see his daughter. When it was time to leave, he secretly gave her some matches so it wouldn't be as dark at night in the castle.

When the bear and his wife returned home, they went to bed. But his wife didn't go to sleep. Instead, she lit a match. She could scarcely believe her eyes. Next to her was not a bear but a handsome prince with a golden crown!

The prince smiled. "Thank you for redeeming me," he said. "I was under an enchantment, and you have now set me free."

Glossary

debt—money owed to other people

distraught—very upset

embroidery—the art of sewing designs on cloth

merchant—someone who carries on a business buying and selling goods

misfortune—bad luck

redeeming—the act of saving someone from something bad

scarcely—hardly

wretched—miserable

Critical Thinking with Common Core

1. Look at the illustrations for "The Fairy Serpent." What details tell you the story takes place in China? (Key Ideas and Details)

2. How do the merchant's actions contribute to the sequence of events in "The Bear Prince?" (Craft and Structure)

3. What does the author mean when she says, "A giant fire roared." (Integration of Knowledge and Ideas)

Writing Prompts

1. Write your own *Beauty and the Beast* story where the genders of the characters are reversed. The "beast" is a girl character put under a spell and the "beauty" is a kind boy that rescues her from enchantment.

2. Write a "Reader's Theater" script of one of the stories in this book.

Read More

Jones, Ursula. *Beauty and the Beast*. Chicago: Albert Whitman, 2014.

Lee, H. Chuku. *Beauty and the Beast*. New York: HarperCollins, 2014.

Loewen, Nancy. *No Lie, I Acted Like a Beast!: The Story of Beauty and the Beast as Told by the Beast* (The Other Side of the Story). North Mankato, Minn.: Picture Window Books, 2013.

Yolen, Jane & Dotlatch, Rebecca Kai. *Grumbles From the Forest: Fairy-Tale Voices with a Twist*. Honesdale, Pa.: Wordsong, 2013.

Internet Sites

FactHound offers a safe, fun way to find Internet sites related to this book. All of the sites on FactHound have been researched by our staff.

Here's all you do:

Visit *www.facthound.com*

Type in this code: 9781479597055

Check out projects, games and lots more at **www.capstonekids.com**

Thanks to our advisers for their expertise and advice:
Maria Tatar, PhD, Chair, Program in Folklore & Mythology

Editor: Penny West
Designer: Ashlee Suker
Creative Director: Nathan Gassman
Production Specialist: Laura Manthe

Picture Window Books are published by Capstone,
1710 Roe Crest Drive, North Mankato, Minnesota 56003
www.capstonepub.com

Library of Congress Cataloging-in-Publication Data
Names: Meister, Cari, author.
Title: Beauty and the beast stories around the world : 3 beloved tales / by Cari Meister.
Other titles: Nonfiction picture books. Multicultural fairy tales.
Description: North Mankato, Minnesota : Capstone Press, [2017] | Series: Nonfiction picture books. Multicultural fairy tales | Summary: Retells the classic French fairy tale of the enchanted beast, and the maiden whose love rescues him, together with two similar tales from China and Switzerland. | Includes bibliographical references
Identifiers: LCCN 2015050458|
ISBN 9781479597055 (library binding) |
ISBN 9781515804147 (pbk.) |
ISBN 9781515804222 (ebook (pdf))
Subjects: LCSH: Beauty and the beast (Tale) | Fairy tales. | Folklore. | CYAC: Fairy tales. | Folkore.
Classification: LCC PZ8.M5183 Be 2017 | DDC 398.209--dc23
LC record available at http://lccn.loc.gov/2015050458

Look for all the books in the series: